Raquela's Seder

For my dear grandpa Isaac Silver who
introduced me to my first seder.
May his memory live on. —J.E.S.

To all those people who still aim at Raquela's
dream of freedom —S.U.

KAR-BEN PUBLISHING®
An imprint of Lerner Publishing Group, Inc.
241 First Avenue North
Minneapolis, MN 55401 USA
Website address: www.karben.com

Main body text set in Truesdell Std.
Typeface provided by Monotype Typography.

Library of Congress Cataloging-in-Publication Data

Names: Stein, Joel Edward, author. | Ugolotti, Sara, 1988– illustrator.
Title: Raquela's seder / Joel Edward Stein ; illustrated by Sara Ugolotti.
Description: Minneapolis, MN : Kar-Ben Publishing, [2022] | Audience: Ages 5–9. | Audience: Grades
    2–3. | Summary: "Raquela yearns to celebrate a Passover seder, but Inquisition-era Spain is a time
    when Jews must hide their religion. Her clever papa, the best fisherman in town, creates a unique
    celebration for his family"— Provided by publisher.
Identifiers: LCCN 2021014674 (print) | LCCN 2021014675 (ebook) | ISBN 9781728424293 |
    ISBN 9781728427966 (paperback) | ISBN 9781728444277 (ebook)
Subjects: CYAC: Passover—Fiction. | Seder—Fiction. | Jews—Spain—Fiction. | Inquisition—Spain—
    Fiction.
Classification: LCC PZ7.1.S743 Raq 2022 (print) | LCC PZ7.1.S743 (ebook) | DDC [E]—dc23

LC record available at https://lccn.loc.gov/2021014674
LC ebook record available at https://lccn.loc.gov/2021014675

Manufactured in China
1-50827-50166-7/24/2021

0322/B1854/A7

Raquela's Seder

Joel Edward Stein

illustrated by **Sara Ugolotti**

KAR-BEN
PUBLISHING

Raquela had a secret. On Friday nights, she followed her parents down to the wine cellar under their house. There, her mother would light Shabbat candles, and her father would say a prayer over the wine. That secret room was the only place the Rivera family could celebrate Shabbat.

In Spain, where Raquela lived, Jews
were forbidden from practicing their religion.
The king and queen punished those who were caught
observing Jewish customs or celebrating Jewish holidays.

But Raquela's parents had told her about the holiday of Passover,
a celebration of freedom that they could speak of only in whispers.
Raquela dreamed of a Passover seder.

One Friday night, Raquela asked her parents,
"Could we have a seder for Passover this year?"

Mamá sighed. "We cannot. If the king's spies found out what we were doing . . ." She couldn't bring herself to say more.

But Papá looked thoughtful.

Raquela's papá was known as the best fisherman in their town. He had one small fishing boat, and he used only one fishing line. But even when other fishermen came back empty-handed, Raquela's papá always came back with fish.

"How is it that you catch so many fish even when others do not, Papá?" Raquela asked.

"To catch a fish," said Papá, "you must be smarter than a fish."

"And to be smarter than a fish," he went on, "you must think like a fish. Clever fish hide in places where fishermen never expect them to be. It is the clever fish that doesn't get caught."

The night before Passover began, Papá asked Mamá to bake flat matzah and mix some dried fruit with nuts and spices. He asked Raquela to collect a basket, a wine goblet, and a tablecloth.

"We will also need an egg," he said. "And one of the bones we saved from last week's dinner. And some parsley and bitter salad greens from the herb garden."

"Why?" asked Raquela.

"You will see," said Papá.

The next day, before sundown,
Raquela and her mamá crept down
to the shore with the basket,
making sure no one was watching.

Papá was waiting in his boat. Raquela and
Mamá climbed in, and Papá lowered the sail.

He headed toward the islands beyond the bay.

"Where are we going, Papá?" Raquela asked in a whisper.

"We are going to have a seder," he answered.

Papá wove the boat this way and that through the waves. Finally, he lowered the sail and dropped the anchor.

"This is my secret fishing place," said Papá.

Raquela grinned. "Who would think to have a seder here?"

"A clever fish," laughed Papá.

"A clever fish that doesn't get caught!" Raquela said.

Papá set a large crate in the middle of the
boat. He took the tablecloth from the
basket and draped it over the crate.

"This will be our seder table," he said.
Then Mamá set out the matzah crackers, the egg, the parsley,
the bone, the fruit mixture, the bitter greens, and the wine.
He drew a small bowl of salt water from the sea.

Raquela listened eagerly as
Papá told a story. "On Passover," he
said, "we remember how the Jewish people lived in
Egypt a long time ago. They were ruled by wicked Pharaoh.
He made the Jewish people work as his slaves."

Papá picked up the parsley and dipped it into the water.

"Now we take a bite of this," he said and chanted a blessing.

"It tastes so salty!" Raquela said.

"Yes," said Papá. "As salty as the tears cried by our ancestors in Egypt. On Passover we remember how precious freedom is. And we remember how the Jewish people gained their freedom from Pharaoh."

Papá read the Four Questions, beginning with
"Why is this night different from all other nights?"
Then he continued with the Passover story.

"The Jewish people had a leader named Moses.
He warned Pharaoh that God would be very angry if Pharaoh
did not let the people go. But Pharaoh would not listen.

"God brought plagues on the people of Egypt. Finally, after the tenth plague, Pharaoh let the Jewish people go."

"And they left so fast that the bread they made for the journey had no time to rise," said Mamá. "That is why we eat matzah."

Raquela looked up at the starry sky.
She imagined Moses leading the Jewish
people out of Egypt to freedom.

Papá filled the wine goblet and raised it. "A long time ago, God freed the Jewish people from slavery in Egypt. Let us hope that one day we will also be free—free to live as Jews."

Papá turned the boat around,
and they sailed for home.

An old fisherman spotted their boat as it came toward shore.
He wondered why Raquela's father had taken his family out to fish.

"This must have been a special night for you!" he called to them.

"Indeed it was," Papá called back.

Raquela looked at her papá and said softly,
"It was a night different from all other nights."

Historical Note

Imagine a place where strangers could enter your home, tell you what to eat, tell you what to wear, and even tell you what religion to practice. But that is what happened during the Spanish Inquisition.

A few years before Christopher Columbus set sail across the Atlantic in 1492, King Ferdinand II and Queen Isabella ruled Spain. They wanted everyone in their kingdom to be Christians like themselves. Those who were not Christian had a choice to convert or leave Spain.

Many Jewish people lived in Spain at that time. Some chose to leave the country rather than convert to Christianity. Those who stayed were called *conversos*. *Conversos* were outwardly Christian, but many practiced their Jewish traditions in secret. They secretly lit candles on Shabbat, celebrated Jewish holidays, and observed other Jewish traditions.

The Sephardic Jews of today trace their rich culture, foods, customs, and even their Ladino language back to their Spanish ancestry.

The Spanish Inquisition lasted more than 350 years, finally ending in 1834.

About Passover

Passover celebrates the exodus of the Israelite slaves from Egypt and the birth of the Jewish people as a nation. The holiday, observed in late March or April, begins with a festive meal called a seder. Families gather to read the Haggadah, a book that tells the story of the Jewish people's historic journey to freedom. Symbolic foods recall the bitterness of slavery, the haste in which the Jews left Egypt, and the joy of freedom.

About the Author
Joel Edward Stein is a former staff writer for CTB/McGraw-Hill. A member of the Society of Children's Book Writers and Illustrators, he lives in Florida with his wife, son, two birds, and a tortoise. His books include *A Hanukkah with Mazel*, *The Pigeon Man*, and *The Capture of Rafael Ortega*.

About the Illustrator
Sara Ugolotti, born and raised in Italy, is a freelance illustrator of children's books. She has a degree in illustration from the International School of Comics in Reggio Emilia, Italy. She loves art, nature, and animals, especially dogs. She lives in Italy.